The
Monsters of
Marble Avenue

The Monsters of Marble Avenue

by Linda Gondosch

Illustrated by Cat Bowman Smith

Little, Brown and Company

Boston   Toronto   London

To my daughter,
Amy

Text copyright © 1988 by Linda Gondosch
Illustrations copyright © 1988 by Little, Brown
and Company (Inc.)

First Paperback Edition

The characters and events portrayed in this book are
fictitious. Any similarity to real persons, living or
dead, is coincidental and not intended by the author.

Library of Congress Cataloging-in-Publication Data

Gondosch, Linda.
    The monsters of Marble Avenue / by Linda Gondosch.
        p.   cm. — (A Springboard book)
    Summary: One mishap after another dogs Luke's attempts to
put on a puppet show.
    HC: ISBN 0-316-31991-0
    PB: ISBN 0-316-31992-9
    [1. Puppets — Fiction.]   I. Title.
PZ7.G587Mo 1988
[E] — dc19   87-26858
                                                        CIP
                                                         AC

Springboard Books and design is a registered trademark
of Little, Brown and Company (Inc.).

                HC: 10 9 8 7 6 5 4 3 2
                PB: 10 9 8 7 6 5 4 3 2 1

                            WOR

Published simultaneously in Canada
by Little, Brown & Company (Canada) Limited

Printed in the United States of America

The
Monsters of
Marble Avenue

1

The Puppet Problem

Luke Palmer pedaled his bicycle down Marble Avenue. He came to a sudden stop in front of Sam Stamper's house. "I'm in big trouble!" he said.

Sam stopped brushing his dog and looked up. "What's the matter?"

"Everything's the matter," moaned Luke. "I was going to be rich, really rich, this Saturday. Now I'm going to be poor. But it's worse than that." He dropped his bike to the ground and plopped down in the grass.

"It was my first real job. Now I can't do it." Luke ran his hands through his curly red hair.

"What are you talking about?" asked Sam.

"I could have made so much money. What am I going to tell Mrs. Bozwell?" Luke threw himself back in the grass and stared at a big gray cloud.

"Mrs. Bozwell?" Sam was confused.

"Mrs. Bozwell wants me to put on a puppet show at Charlie's little sister Erin's birthday party. I told her I would," explained Luke.

"So what's the problem?"

"I can't," said Luke. "I promised her a puppet show and I can't do it."

"Why not?" asked Sam.

"I don't have any puppets!"

Sam laughed. "You have lots of puppets, Luke. There's a whole boxful in your basement." He continued brushing Rex, his Great Dane.

4

"I *did* have puppets. But not anymore. My mother sold them at her garage sale."

Sam stopped brushing.

"They were in a box of clothes. She sold them by mistake."

"Can you get them back?" Sam asked.

"My mom doesn't remember who bought them," said Luke. "What am I going to do?"

"Tell Charlie's mother you can't give the puppet show," said Sam.

"I can't do that." Luke sat up. "I *promised* her. Anyway, she was going to pay me two dollars. Two whole dollars! Just for a little puppet show. She said she wanted Erin's party to be special. She's counting on me."

Sam picked a flea off Rex as he thought a moment. "No problem," he finally said. "We'll go down to Beekman's Store and buy some puppets. They're having a big sale."

"They are?"

"I've got a little money. I'll help you out," said Sam.

"You will?"

"Sure. Come on." Sam hopped onto his bike and whistled for Rex.

"But I've only got a quarter," said Luke. He picked up his bike.

"No problem," said Sam. "They're on sale. They won't cost very much. Let's go."

"I hope they still have some," said Luke. "What if they're all sold out?"

"Then you *are* in trouble," said Sam.

Luke and Sam bicycled down Marble Avenue as fast as they could go.

2

Gorilla Girls

"Stay!" said Sam. He pointed at the side-walk. Rex sat down and whined. Luke wished he had a big dog like Rex. He would teach him all sorts of tricks. But his parents always said no. Oh, well, thought Luke, now I have another problem. He'd have to worry about how to get a dog some other day.

The boys leaned their bikes against the front of Beekman's Store and walked inside. They passed the candy counter and the school sup-plies counter before they saw the puppets.

There were big puppets and little puppets,

puppets with cloth outfits and plastic faces and silky hair. Staring up at Luke and Sam were monsters and monkeys, boys and girls, ducks, donkeys, doctors, martians, princesses, kings, babies, and rabbits. Oh, I could give the most fantastic show ever with puppets like these, thought Luke.

Luke reached for a fuzzy brown bear puppet. "I like this one. I want to do 'Goldilocks and the Three Bears.' This puppet would make a perfect Papa Bear." He slid it onto his hand and wiggled his fingers.

"Who's been sleeping in my bed?" Luke growled, as he bounced his puppet up and down.

"Put it back," said Sam. "Let's go."

"Huh?" Luke stopped working his puppet. "I need puppets, Sam. I have an important show to give in just four days."

"You'd better look at the price," said Sam. He pointed to a sign.

"Six ninety-five!" said Luke. His heart sank. He wanted the puppet so much. But four puppets would be much too expensive. They were almost seven dollars apiece. Luke did some quick figuring. "Twenty-eight dollars, Sam! I don't have twenty-eight cents."

He put the bear puppet back on the counter. "I thought you said puppets don't cost that much."

"I was wrong," said Sam.

"May I help you?" asked a clerk.

"I wish you could," said Luke. He looked back at the puppets one last time as he slowly walked away.

"BOO!"

Luke jumped. Melissa Diller and Annie Thorp had popped up from behind the school supplies counter. They held out their hands like claws and made their scariest faces.

"Annie!" said Luke. "Do you have to jump out at me everywhere I go?"

"Oh, now, Luke," scolded Annie. She swatted her short black hair from her eyes. "Don't be such a baby."

"Yikes!" hollered Sam. "Monster girls. Gorilla girls. Geeky, freaky girls! Let's get out of here fast." Sam grabbed Luke's shoulder and practically dragged him to the door.

Melissa and Annie chased after them. "Rex!" called Annie. "My favorite dog. Here, boy!" Rex jumped on Annie and knocked her to the sidewalk.

"Get down, Rex," ordered Sam.

Annie laughed. "Down, boy!"

"What were you doing in Beekman's?" Melissa asked Luke.

"Looking at puppets," said Luke.

"Gonna have a puppet show?" asked Annie, scrambling to her feet.

"I *was*," answered Luke, "but I don't have twenty-eight dollars. Those puppets cost too much."

"Come on, Luke," yelled Sam, already pedaling away. "We don't talk to girls."

"See you later," said Luke. He called for Rex as he rode off.

"Come back here," ordered Annie. "I know how you can have a puppet show. Hey!"

But Luke didn't hear her. He pumped as hard as he could down Marble Avenue. "Wait for me, Sam!"

3

A Two-Dollar Deal

"Now what are we going to do?" asked Luke as he and Sam parked the bicycles in Luke's driveway. "I still don't have any puppets."

"We're going to hide," said Sam. "The gorilla girls might have followed us."

"They're not so bad," said Luke, but he followed Sam into the garage and pulled down the door.

"I'll never get any puppets," said Luke. "And Charlie's mom is counting on me."

"Forget about the puppets, will you?" said Sam. "I never had a puppet show at my birthday party."

"But Mrs. Bozwell was going to pay me two dollars."

"Who cares?" said Sam.

"I care! I could go into the puppet-show business and give shows at every party on the street. I could be a millionaire by next year," said Luke.

"Forget it," said Sam. "Shhh! I hear someone."

They stood on tiptoe and peeked out the garage-door windows. Hedy, Luke's four-year-old sister, was pushing her baby stroller down the sidewalk. She stopped as Annie and Melissa ran up to her.

"Hey, Hedy," called Annie. "Have you seen Luke and Sam?"

"Maybe," said Hedy.

"I see their bikes," said Melissa. "They can't be far."

"They're not far," said Hedy.

"Where did they go?" asked Annie, looking around.

"Not telling. Not ever. Never!" said Hedy.

"Give up," said Melissa. "Hedy doesn't know anything. She's too little."

"You're right. Let's ask someone else," said Annie.

"I am *not* too little!" said Hedy. She pointed to her house. "They're in the garage."

"Way to go, Hedy," whispered Sam. "We're dead ducks, Luke. Let's get out of here." Sam raced to the back door of the garage. It was locked.

"I don't know what you're so afraid of," said Luke. "I'm letting them in." He lifted the garage door and stood facing Annie and Melissa.

"You are not very nice, Luke Palmer," said Annie.

"Don't ever call us monster girls again!" said Melissa.

"I didn't say that," said Luke. "Sam did."

"I ought to tell your mother on you, Sam," said Annie. "I ought to not tell you how to make puppets. I ought to — "

"Wait," said Luke. "You know how to make puppets?"

"Sure I do. But I'm not telling you," said Annie.

"I'll pay you," cried Luke.

"How much?" asked Annie.

"A nickel," said Luke. Annie whispered to Melissa. Then they both ran down the driveway.

"Don't go!" called Luke. "You've got to show me how to make puppets. I have to give a puppet show for Erin Bozwell's birthday party on Saturday. I need puppets."

Annie whispered to Melissa again. Melissa smiled.

"I'm getting paid two whole dollars. It's my first real job," said Luke.

"Let's make a deal," said Annie. "I'll show you how to make puppets if you and I and Melissa get to put on the show. We'll split the money."

"Hey, what about me?" said Sam. "I want in on this, too."

Luke folded his arms across his chest and thought. Two dollars split four ways was only fifty cents apiece. But he could sure use the help. Also, putting on a show with his friends would be much more fun than doing it all by himself.

"Okay, it's a deal," Luke said. He and Annie slapped hands. "Now, how do we make puppets? I want a Goldilocks puppet and three bear puppets."

Annie whooped with joy. "Okay, you get a bucket of water and a bunch of old newspapers. Bring a bag of flour and any old toilet-paper tubes you can find. I'll get my sewing box."

"Toilet-paper tubes? What for?" asked Luke.

"For necks. They make great puppet necks." Annie and Melissa ran to Annie's house next door.

"Way to go, Luke," grumbled Sam. "Why did you open the garage door?"

18

4

Messy, Mushy Muck

"Without them we could have kept all the money ourselves," Sam said.

"Without them we wouldn't have any puppets," Luke said.

Sam thought a moment. "I have an idea! We'll get Annie to help us make the puppets, and then we'll give the show ourselves, just you and I, Luke."

"That's not fair. What's wrong with Annie and Melissa anyway?"

"I'll tell you what's wrong. Show-off Annie

19

has to boss everyone around like she's queen or something, and Melissa's a crybaby."

"She is not."

"She is, too. Remember when she fell in the puddle on the playground and screamed for two hours? She acts like dirt is poison. Geek girls."

"Well, I like them," said Luke. "And this is my house."

Just then Annie and Melissa came in, carrying a cardboard box between them. "Where are the newspapers?" asked Melissa.

"Right here." Luke pointed to a stack of old newspapers in the corner of the garage. "I'll be right back with the flour." He ran inside his house.

"Where's the bucket of water?" asked Annie.

"Here's a bucket," said Sam. "Go get some water." He handed the bucket to Annie.

"You get it," said Annie. "I have to figure out what cloth to use." Sam yanked the bucket back and stomped out of the garage.

It wasn't long before everyone was gathered on the floor of the garage. They tore the newspapers into skinny strips. Annie dumped some flour into the bucket of water. Sam and Luke squished their hands up and down in the bucket until a thick paste formed.

"Now for the fun part." Annie crumpled some paper into a little ball and poked it onto the end of a toilet-paper tube. She tied it with a string to hold it tight. Then she dumped the shredded newspaper strips into the paste. She pulled out long, mushy strips and wrapped them around and around the newspaper ball.

"Keep adding paper strips around the ball until you have a nice round head. See? This is called papier-mâché."

"I call it a mess," said Melissa. "Do I have to stick my hands in this muck?"

"If you want a puppet, you do," said Annie. She smoothed and squeezed the papier-mâché ball until it looked like a round head with a

chin. Then she pasted a little wet blob in the middle of the ball. "That's the nose."

"Hey, I see it!" called Luke.

"How do you make the eyes?" asked Sam. He peered over Annie's shoulder.

"We'll paint those on later," said Annie.

Soon they were all making papier-mâché heads. Sam's head was the biggest of all. He added a huge nose. "This is Papa Bear. I'll paint his nose black."

He stuck the wet head on his finger and held it over the bucket of mush. "Who has been eating my porridge?" he snarled. In his own voice he said, "This looks just like the oatmeal I had for breakfast. Yuck!" Papa Bear's head slid off Sam's finger and plopped on the floor.

"Good job, Sam," said Luke. "You just smashed Papa Bear's nose."

5

The Great Papier-Mâché Fight

After they were finished, they laid the puppet heads in a row on Luke's driveway.

"These will take a while to dry," said Annie.

"I hope they dry fast. We only have four days," said Luke.

"When they're dry," continued Annie, "we'll paint faces with poster paint."

They all stood back and looked at the four puppet heads drying on the driveway. "They look sort of sick to me," said Melissa.

"That's because they're wet," said Annie. "They'll look better after they dry."

"You know what we could do?" said Luke. "We could turn this into a puppet theater." He walked to the corner of the garage. A small nook with three walls extended back from the rest of the garage. The nook had a window with a torn screen.

"We could hang a sheet across here, and this window could be our puppet stage. Everyone could sit on the grass and watch," said Luke. "What do you think?"

"No way!" said Melissa. "This place is too messy. We would have to clean it first. Look at those dirty old dead bugs." She pointed to the ceiling.

"We could pull out these boxes and the lawn mower. I don't think Dad would mind."

"In between shows we could make hundreds of puppets and sell them!" said Annie. "Oh, Luke, what a terrific idea!"

"I think it stinks," said Sam.

"Oh, Sam, you never want to do anything," said Annie.

"Oh, yes, I do," said Sam. "I like to do a lot of things. I like to play baseball and miniature golf — "

"Let's go play miniature golf after the puppet show," interrupted Annie. "I bet I would win again."

"You never won the last time," said Sam. "That game was no fair. I would have won if my golf club hadn't been crooked."

Melissa laughed. "Your club wasn't crooked. You just can't hit a ball."

"I can, too."

"Come on, Sam," said Luke. "Annie beat us fair and square. You know she did."

"She did not!" said Sam.

"I did, too!" said Annie.

Suddenly Sam reached over and scooped up a glob of newspaper mush from the bucket. He smeared it in Annie's face.

26

"Ha!" shouted Sam. "How do you like that?"

Melissa screamed.

"Sam, are you crazy?" hollered Luke.

Annie blinked her eyes and opened her mouth wide. A hunk of wet goop slid down her nose and dropped off.

"Sam! Look what you did!" spluttered Annie.

"Ha, ha! Now you *really* look like a monster," said Sam.

Annie dug into the mush. Sam raced out of the garage. He grabbed his bike and pedaled down the driveway as fast as he could go. Annie flung a handful of papier-mâché. It landed with a splat on Sam's neck.

Sam turned around. "See if I ever help you put on a puppet show!" he yelled.

"See if we care," said Annie.

"Come on, Annie," said Luke. "At least we still have his puppet."

"We can do the show without him," said Melissa. "We'll find someone else to play Papa Bear."

They walked back to the garage. A blue car was turning into the driveway from Marble Avenue.

"Dad!" yelled Luke. "Stop!"

Squish. The car ran over the four puppet heads.

6

The Marble Avenue Club

Mr. Palmer got out of the car with a bright smile on his face. "Hi, kids!" he called.

"Dad, you just ran over Goldilocks!" cried Luke. He pointed toward the car wheels.

Mr. Palmer's smile disappeared. He dropped a bag of groceries. "I did what?"

"You ran over Goldilocks and the three bears," said Luke. "Our puppets. Look at them!"

Mr. Palmer looked. The papier-mâché heads looked like lumpy gray pancakes. "I'm sorry," he said. "I didn't see anything. What did you say that was?"

"It *was* our puppets," groaned Luke. "Now what am I going to do?"

"What am *I* going to do?" said Annie. "My face is getting hard. I'm going to crack!"

"What's on your face?" asked Luke's father.

"Papier-mâché," said Annie. She wiped her face with her sleeve. Melissa tried not to laugh. She covered her mouth.

"How can you laugh at a time like this?" said Luke. "Our puppets just died."

"Yeah, but look how funny Annie looks," said Melissa.

Luke's father picked up the groceries and went inside. Luke scraped up the flattened puppet heads with a snow shovel. He dumped them into a garbage can.

"Don't worry, Luke," said Annie. "We can make more."

"Tomorrow," said Luke. "Tomorrow after

school we'll have our first puppet-making meeting in the corner of the garage."

The next day Luke, Melissa, and Annie cleaned out the corner of the garage. "Dad felt bad about running over our puppets," said Luke. "That's why he said we could fix this place up." He swept the floor with a broom and swatted at the dead bugs hanging from the ceiling.

"I brought a rug. It's small, but it will do," said Annie as she rolled out a tattered red rug. Luke brought in a small table and some chairs and a lamp with a crooked shade. An old, scratched kitchen cabinet was pushed under the window. The cabinet would be perfect for storing puppet supplies.

"We need a curtain," said Melissa.

"No curtains," said Luke. "That window is our puppet stage, remember? Curtains will get in the way."

"Mom let me have this sheet," said Annie.

She held up an old yellow sheet with a hole in it. Luke tied a rope from one wall to another. Annie and Melissa threw the sheet over the rope. It completely hid the corner from the rest of the garage. They pulled back the sheet and went inside.

"Hey, look," said Annie. She put her eye up to the hole in the sheet. "We have our own private peephole. We can make sure no one is spying on us."

"Who'd want to spy on us?" asked Melissa.

"Someone who wanted a preview of the best puppet show ever," said Luke.

Luke, Melissa, and Annie spent the rest of the afternoon making four more puppet heads. This time they put them back on the patio to dry. They weren't taking any more chances with cars. Annie spread scraps of blue, red, and yellow cloth on the table. "Puppet bodies," said Melissa. "I want yellow." They drew dresses with sleeves and then cut them out.

"Now you have to sew around the edge," explained Annie. "When you're done, turn it inside out."

"I can't sew this," said Luke.

"Nothing to it," said Annie. "Just don't sew across the neck. Later we'll fasten that to the toilet paper tube with a rubber band. It's easy."

The kitchen telephone rang. "Luke! It's for you," called his mother. "It's Mrs. Bozwell."

"Hello, Luke," said Mrs. Bozwell. "I just want to know how the puppet show is coming along. You haven't forgotten, have you?"

"Don't worry about a thing," said Luke. "I've got everything under control. This will be the best puppet show ever."

"Good, good," said Mrs. Bozwell. "Erin can't wait to see it. Remember, Saturday at one o'clock."

Luke returned to the clubhouse and told

Annie and Melissa about the telephone call. After that, they worked even harder on the puppets.

No one noticed how late it was until Melissa's mother called her. Before Melissa left, they ran to the patio to check on the puppet heads.

"Where did they go?" cried Melissa.

"We put them right here," said Luke.

"They're gone!" said Annie.

7

A Mysterious Gravy Path

Luke's sister, Hedy, was swinging on her swing set and eating a banana. "Hedy!" called Luke. "Have you seen our puppet heads?"

Hedy took a bite of banana and chewed slowly. She looked at the sky.

"Hedy!"

"Yes," she answered with her mouth full of banana.

"What did you do with them?" asked Luke. "Hurry!"

"I fixed them."

"You what?"

"I painted them," said Hedy. "Albert helped me." Albert was in Hedy's nursery-school class.

"Oh, wonderful," said Luke.

"Our puppets are ruined!" cried Annie. "You absolutely cannot paint them till they're dry."

Hedy's smile faded. She looked as if she were about to cry. "I wanted to help, Luke. I just wanted to help."

Luke almost felt sorry for his sister, but then he thought of the puppet show. Only three days away and still he had no puppets. How could he give a puppet show without puppets?

"How did you paint them, Hedy?" asked Luke. "Did you get into my paint set?"

"Nope," said Hedy. She took another bite of banana and looked at her tennis shoes.

"How did you paint them?" repeated Luke.

"With gravy," said Hedy.

"Quit talking with banana in your mouth," said Luke. "With what?"

"With gravy. I thought gravy would make nice brown bears. I put yellow M&M's for eyes. They were pretty."

Annie fell on the ground. "That's just great. Gravy bears. What were you going to do, eat them for dinner?"

Melissa smacked her forehead. "Well, that's that. We might as well give up. I'm going home."

"I ought to paint *you* with gravy, Hedy," shouted Luke. "That is the dumbest thing I ever heard."

"It is not!" Hedy burst out crying. She threw her banana peel at Luke's shoe. "I wanted to help. I wanted to be in your club, too."

"What club?" Luke asked. "We don't have a club."

"Yes, you do!" said Hedy. "In the garage."

"I guess you could call it a club." Luke

suddenly pictured himself as a club president. It felt good.

"So where are the puppets?" Annie asked Hedy.

"I don't know," said Hedy.

"Where did you put them?" asked Luke.

"On the patio," said Hedy. "I don't know where they went." She ran inside the house.

Luke and Annie walked Melissa home. As they were passing Sam's house, Luke spotted something in the grass.

"Look at this!" he said.

"A yellow M&M!" cried Annie. They searched the ground.

"Look what I found," said Melissa. She picked up a chunk of wet papier-mâché. It was dripping with gravy.

"These are our puppets!" said Luke.

"*Were* our puppets," said Annie. "I bet I know who took them."

"I can't believe it. Our good friend Sam is a puppet thief," said Luke.

"It sure looks that way," said Melissa. She followed a path of papier-mâché around Sam's house.

"Here's another M&M," called Annie. She reached into the garden.

A window flew open. "You kids stay out of my garden!" yelled Mrs. Stamper. "I told you that before, didn't I?" Sam's mother was not the friendliest mother on the street.

"Is Sam home?" asked Luke.

Sam came to the window. His mother left. "What do you want?"

"We just want our puppets back," said Luke. "You didn't have to tear them into a thousand pieces."

"I didn't tear them into a thousand pieces," said Sam.

"You're lying," said Annie. "You took our puppets and — " Sam slammed the window and pulled the curtain.

"Don't worry," said Melissa. "We'll think of something, Luke."

"Sure," said Luke. He knew there was no chance of ever giving a puppet show for Erin's birthday party. He knew he would never get paid for his first real job. He was a failure.

Rex stood beside his doghouse and barked. "I guess I'll say goodnight to Rex," said Annie. "Race you to the doghouse."

Annie, Melissa, and Luke ran to the doghouse. They couldn't believe what they saw when they got there.

8

Puppet Thief

Rex was chomping on the remains of a puppet head. He looked up, wagged his tail, and licked his lips.

"So *you* are the puppet thief!" said Luke.

"Oh, Rex, how could you do such a bad thing?" said Annie. "You're not my favorite dog anymore. Bad!"

"I hope you enjoyed your dinner," said Melissa. Rex wagged his tail and returned to the puppet.

"And you thought *I* stole the puppets,"

said a voice from behind them. Luke, Melissa, and Annie spun around. Sam stood with his hands on his hips.

"We were wrong," said Luke. "Sorry, Sam."

"Is that all you can say?" said Sam.

"You can be in our club," Luke offered.

"What club?" Sam asked.

"Maybe we don't want him in our club," said Melissa.

"Maybe I don't want to be in your club," said Sam. "What do you do, make puppets all day?"

"We do lots of things," said Luke, thinking hard. "Like hold meetings."

"And make decisions," Annie joined in.

"And collect money," said Melissa.

"Money?" asked Sam.

"The money we make from putting on puppet shows," Luke said.

"Could I be president?" Sam asked.

"I'm president," Luke said quickly, "since the club meets in my garage."

"And I'm vice-president," Annie decided.

"Forget it!" said Sam.

"You could be treasurer, Sam," Luke suggested. "You like to count money."

While Sam was making up his mind, Melissa saw something move in the grass. "Eeek!"

she screamed, picking up her feet. "A thousand-legger!"

"I can't stand it! She's afraid of a little thousand-legger," said Sam. "I'm not joining any club with wimpy girls." He grabbed Luke's shoulders and whispered, "Let's make our own club. Just you and I. We could get Charlie, too."

"If I can't be in the club, I'm taking my sheet back. And my rug!" said Annie.

Luke held his head in his hands. "Why can't you just be friends? All I wanted to do was put on one little puppet show . . ."

"And *his* dog ruined it!" said Melissa, glaring at Sam.

"The puppet show is off, Luke," said Annie. "I quit. You'd better tell Mrs. Bozwell. Tonight."

On Thursday Luke called an emergency meeting of the Marble Avenue Club, minus Sam. First he showed Annie and Melissa a sign he had made.

"Ring what bell?" asked Annie.

Luke pulled a small bell from his pocket and rang it. "This bell." He placed it on a shelf just outside the sheet. Then he said, "We've still got time. I think we can do it."

"You mean you didn't call Mrs. Bozwell?" asked Annie. "She still thinks there's going to be a puppet show?"

"There *is* going to be a puppet show," said Luke. "Mom got me another bag of flour. I've got tons of newspapers. Mom said we could dry the puppets in the oven this time." Luke held up the stitched puppet dresses. "These are almost finished. And we still have tomorrow to practice." He stopped when he heard a bell ringing.

"Someone's here," whispered Annie. "She peeked through the hole in the sheet. "Guess who!"

"Who?" asked Luke and Melissa.

"Sam."

The bell rang again. Luke pulled back the sheet. Sam walked in with some newspapers under one arm and a bag of flour under the other.

"I want to join the club," he said. "If I help you make new puppets, can I join?" He dumped the heavy bag of flour and the newspapers on the table.

"I thought you didn't want to," said Annie.

"I changed my mind."

Luke looked quickly at Annie and Melissa. "No more papier-mâché fights?"

"No more. I promise."

"No more calling us monster girls?" said Annie.

"Okay, okay," said Sam. "I gave Rex a good talking to last night. He howled all night. I think he had a bellyache after eating those puppets."

9

Erin Bozwell's Birthday Bash

For the next few hours the Marble Avenue clubhouse was a busy place. A new batch of papier-mâché was made. Puppet heads were shaped, even better than before. They were carefully placed in the oven to dry. Puppet clothes were sewn. Lines for the play were practiced.

By Saturday, the puppets were ready. They lay in a box in the clubhouse. Eyes and red smiling mouths had been painted on their faces. Goldilocks's head was covered with long yellow yarn. The three bears had brown furry heads. Annie had cut pieces of fur from her sister's old slippers.

"I asked Mrs. Bozwell if we could have the show in our theater," said Luke. He pointed to the clubhouse window. "She said it was okay. I think she liked the idea of everyone coming here for a while."

Annie carried a chair outside, climbed onto it, and posted a sign over the window.

Almost everyone from Erin Bozwell's kindergarten class was at the party. Charlie Bozwell met Luke, Sam, Annie, and Melissa at the door. "The puppet show people are here!"

he called. "Come on in and have some hot dogs. We're not ready for the show yet."

"Oh, good," said Melissa, hurrying inside. "I'm starved."

Mrs. Bozwell ran around saying, "So glad you came! Put the presents on the table. Wipe your feet on the mat. Oh, don't you look pretty! Turn on the music, Charlie. Do you want to play games first or eat first?"

"Eat!" shouted everyone at once.

All the party-goers gathered around the dining-room table and sang "Happy Birthday." They gobbled up chocolate cake, hot dogs and mustard, potato chips, pretzels, pink lemonade, and root beer. Luke and his friends ate with Charlie at a separate table. They were glad they didn't have to mingle with the little kids. And they even got their own bags of candy.

Luke and Annie put their candy in their pockets. Melissa and Sam ate every bite of their lemon drops, candy kisses, and chocolate bars.

"I heard you have a club," said Charlie. "Can I join?"

Luke looked at Sam, Annie, and Melissa. "I don't know, Charlie. Maybe."

"I'll bring potato chips. Mom always buys potato chips." Charlie crunched and munched a large potato chip. "What do you say?"

"Sounds good to me," said Melissa.

"Sure," said Annie. "We'll let you join."

"Don't forget the chips," said Sam.

Right after the balloon-popping contest Melissa said, "I don't feel so good." Her face was green. "I'm going to be sick." She flew out the front door and ran home.

"Wait!" called Luke. "You can't leave. Come back here, Melissa. We need you!"

"We want the show! We want the show!" yelled all the party-goers.

"I think it's time for the puppet show,"

said Mrs. Bozwell. "Why don't you all head over to your garage, Luke?"

"Give us a head start," said Luke, "so we can get ready."

The Marble Avenue Club had another emergency meeting backstage. A noisy crowd gathered outside.

"What will we do without Melissa?" asked Luke.

"Who's going to play Baby Bear?"

"How about Hedy?" Annie suggested.

"Hedy can't be Baby Bear," said Sam. "She'll ruin the show."

"I will not," said Hedy. She licked her ice cream.

"You'll have to give your cone to someone and wash your hands," said Luke.

"Okay, Luke!" cried Hedy happily. She handed her ice cream cone to Albert Krog. "Don't lick it," she told him. Then she ran to wash her hands.

"Hedy can't reach the window," said Sam. "She's too short."

"Yes, I can," said Hedy as she hurried into the clubhouse. "I'll climb up on this cabinet."

"Do you know what Baby Bear is supposed to say?" asked Luke.

"Of course I do," said Hedy. "I've heard that story before."

"We want the show!" shouted the audience.

10

Head-Over-Heels Hedy

Luke, Sam, Annie, and Hedy slipped the puppets on their hands. The three bears walked across the windowsill. Everyone became quiet.

"I want to go for a walk in the woods!" squealed Baby Bear. "My porridge is too hot." Hedy danced her puppet left and right. Baby Bear suddenly flew off Hedy's hand and landed in Jeremy Jolson's lap.

"Wow! Baby Bear's porridge must have been really hot," said Jeremy. Everyone laughed.

Hedy popped up. Jeremy waved the puppet in the air.

"Give me back my puppet," said Hedy.

"Come and get it," called Jeremy. Hedy climbed higher on the cabinet and reached out the window. She tried to reach her puppet.

"Give it to me, Jeremy!" she said. She reached too far. Head over heels, Hedy tumbled out the window. She landed with a thud on top of Albert Krog.

"Ouch, my arm!" hollered Albert. Hedy let out a loud wail.

"Are you all right?" asked Luke. He leaned out the window.

Hedy suddenly stopped crying. "What's this?" she said. She pulled a strawberry ice cream cone from the seat of her pants. "My ice cream cone!" she cried. "Oh, Albert."

"It's not *my* fault," said Albert.

As soon as everyone saw that Hedy was

not hurt, they began to laugh. Hedy went back to Charlie's house for another ice cream cone.

Luke played the parts of Mama Bear and Baby Bear. Now and then he became confused and said Mama Bear's line with Baby Bear's voice, but the audience loved it. When the three bears chased Goldilocks from the house, everyone applauded.

"We want more! We want more!" they cried when the show ended. So Luke, Annie, and Sam made up another show. This show was about three ugly monsters and a schoolteacher with long yellow hair. The kids liked the monster story even more than "Goldilocks and the Three Bears."

When he finally returned to Charlie's house, Luke felt wonderful. The show had been a success, except for Hedy's accident.

"How was the show?" asked Mrs. Bozwell.

"Super!" said Jeremy Jolson. "You should have seen Hedy fall out the window."

"Best show I ever saw," said two or three others.

Charlie's mother turned to Luke. "Thanks, Luke, for a job well done. You and your puppeteers really made Erin's party special. Here are your two dollars, and a one-dollar bonus." She handed Luke some coins.

"A bonus? Thanks!" Luke looked at the extra money.

"For Hedy's fall," said Mrs. Bozwell.

Luke gave fifty cents apiece to Sam and Annie. Hedy held out her hand and he gave her fifty cents.

"Thanks, Luke," said Hedy.

"I'll give Melissa fifty cents, too, okay?"

"Yeah," agreed Annie and Sam. "She earned it."

"Whatever is left over goes into our club's bank," said Luke.

"Our club! In all the excitement, I almost forgot," said Annie. "There's so much to look forward to: holding meetings, making decisions . . ."

"Spending money," Sam continued. "What should we buy?"

"I don't know," Luke said. "Maybe we could have some T-shirts made with our club name on them. The Marble Avenue Club."

"That's a boring name for a club," said Annie.

"Do you have any better ideas?" said Sam.

"As a matter of fact, I do," Annie said, smiling at Sam. "How about the Marble Avenue Monsters?"

"I like it!" said Sam.

"We'll vote on that tomorrow," said Luke. "Right now I want a strawberry ice cream cone."